DATE DUE			
AG 29 '89			
MY 17 '90			
JY 31 '90			
OC 20 '90			

Amazing Ghosts & Other Mysteries

Peter Eldin
Illustrated by Kim Blundell

 Sterling Publishing Co., Inc.   New York

2321537

Library of Congress Cataloging-in-Publication Data

Eldin, Peter.
   [Amazing ghosts and ghouls. Selections]
   Amazing ghosts & other mysteries / by Peter Eldin ; illustrated by
Kim Blundell.
       p.   cm.
   "Compiled and adapted from Amazing ghosts and ghouls and Amazing
mysteries and phenomena"—T.p. verso.
   Includes index.
   Summary: Recounts ghost stories both funny and frightening, about
poltergeists, animal ghosts, and phantom skulls, and also tales of
unexplained and mysterious phenomena, miracles, appearances, and
disappearances.
   ISBN 0-8069-6886-9
   1. Ghosts—Juvenile literature. [1. Ghosts. 2. Curiosities and
wonders.] I. Blundell, Kim, ill. II. Eldin, Peter. Amazing
mysteries and phenomena. Selections. 1988. III. Title.
IV. Title: Amazing ghosts and other mysteries.
BF1461.E4325 1988
133.1—dc19   88-10191
                                                                   CIP
                                                                    AC

Published in 1988 by Sterling Publishing Co., Inc.
Two Park Avenue, New York, New York 10016
The material in this book was compiled and adapted from
Amazing Ghosts and Ghouls and *Amazing Mysteries
and Phenomena* published in Great Britain by
Octopus Books Limited.
Copyright © 1987 Octopus Books Limited.
Distributed in Canada by Oak Tree Press Ltd.
% Canadian Manda Group, P.O. Box 920
Station U, Toronto, Ontario M8Z 5P9
Manufactured in the United States of America

Contents

By the Same Author
Amazing Pranks & Blunders

To the Reader

Have you ever seen a ghost?

If you haven't—hold onto your seat! This book is crammed with ghosts and ghouls of all kinds: ghosts from the depths of the sea, pesky poltergeists, ghosts that haunt houses and theaters, animal ghosts, phantom skulls and ghoulish skeletons.

You'll also find mysteries that have perplexed people for centuries and may never be solved— strange tales of odd animals and monsters, incredible miracles, peculiar appearances and unexplained disappearances.

Do you want to be baffled, bewildered and befuddled? Are your nerves strong enough? Read on and find out.

1 · That's Peculiar!

A Smelly Ghost

Footsteps have been heard frequently in Orcas Manor, in Dorset, England. The ghostly footsteps are often accompanied by a noise that sounds like a body being dragged along the ground. But, even stranger is the fact that after the noise has stopped, there is a lingering, putrid smell that no one can account for.

The Phantom Fowl

One of the most unusual phantoms on record is the ghostly chicken seen in Highgate, London. The chicken appears and then suddenly vanishes. But the strangest thing about this phantom fowl is that it is half-plucked!

Suicide Song

In 1935 Lazzlo Javor, a Hungarian poet, wrote a song called "Gloomy Sunday." It was later put to music by Rezsoe Seres and the record became a hit.

Lazzlo Javor's former girlfriend, for whom the song had been written, committed suicide shortly after the record was released. Her suicide note said, "Gloomy Sunday." A short while later a Hungarian government official shot himself. He was found slumped over a copy of the lyrics of

"Gloomy Sunday." Next, a girl tried to poison herself. When she was found, "Gloomy Sunday" was still playing on the phonograph in the room. In a Budapest restaurant a young man shot himself—the band had just played "Gloomy Sunday."

The Hungarian government thought the situation was getting out of hand, so they banned all public performances of the song. In England, where other suicides had been reported, the BBC also banned it. Similar suicides were reported in the U.S., but the government decided against banning the song.

In all, there were some 200 suicides around the world that were said to be connected with "Gloomy Sunday." Then, in 1968, a Hungarian jumped to his death from the eighth floor of a building. It was Rezsoe Seres, who had never been able to write another hit after "Gloomy Sunday."

In-Flight Disaster

In January 1969, a squadron of ducks, flying over the county of St. Marys, Maryland, appeared to crash into an invisible barrier. No one heard or saw the strange accident, but hundreds of birds fell to the ground. They had suffered broken bones and extensive bleeding. Examination of the dead birds proved that these injuries had been caused before the birds hit the ground. They must have hit something in mid-air—but what?

Don't Bring Your Dog

The spirit of Sir Francis Drake is said to ride across the moors in Devon, with a ghostly pack of hounds alongside him. Supposedly, any dog who hears the hounds is destined to die immediately.

Everybody Wants to Get into the Act!

During the performance of a play at a theatre in Surrey, England in 1973, many people in the audience were puzzled about why one actor remained in the shadows during the performance, taking no active part in the show.

It puzzled the producer even more, because he hadn't cast any such actor in his play. Furthermore, the doorway in which people saw the man standing did not even exist!

The ghost appeared on subsequent evenings, and 24 people from four performances said they saw him. Everyone who described him said he was dressed in 16th-century clothing. But who the man was, and why he wanted to take part in the performance, remains a mystery.

Star Sign

Sirius, the brightest star in the night sky, has a companion star, Sirius B. The Dogon, a remote tribe in Africa, have made drawings of Sirius and Sirius B. But Sirius B is so faint it can be seen only with a very powerful telescope, and the Dogon had no telescopes at all. To date, no one has been able to figure out how the Dogon knew about Sirius B when it cannot be seen with the naked eye!

The Polite Ghost

The ghost of a nun goes around knocking on bedroom doors in Ripley Castle, Yorkshire. She is very polite, however. She only enters the room if the occupant says: "Come in."

Neat Ghost!

In 1975, the Usher family of East London was amazed by the antics of a ghost in their house. She would slam doors and often cause a terrible commotion. She was also very abusive at times, especially to a psychic investigator who was called in to get rid of her. The ghost did have one useful trait, however—she enjoyed doing housework. The Ushers did not have to make the beds, tidy their closets or clean the bathroom—the ghost did it all for them.

R-Rated Ghost

The Cauld (Cold) Lad is the ghost of Hylton Castle in England. Thought to be the ghost of a stable boy who was killed in the castle, he is rather an unusual phantom—he appears naked!

Stone Giants

All over Easter Island in the South Pacific are giant stone statues. No one knows who carved them or why.

The island was discovered by Dutch admiral Jacob Roggeveen on Easter Sunday 1722. Approaching the island he thought he had found a land of giants—but the giants turned out to be enormous carved stone heads. There were almost 300 of them, measuring 12 feet tall and weighing over 55 tons.

Scientists have since examined the statues, but have been unable to explain how they came to be there. The statues were carved inside the crater of the dormant volcano Rano Raraku and then moved, but no one has worked out how the natives managed to get them from the crater to their present places.

Horse in the Lake

Patrick Canning was standing on the shore of Lake Shanakeever in County Galway, Ireland, one day in 1955. He saw a white horse on the shore and walked towards it to take a closer look. The horse seemed to have an unusually long neck, but apart from that it seemed ordinary. As he approached, the creature plunged into the lake and disappeared beneath the surface.

Several other people have seen a white horse plunging into Lake Shanakeever, and no one has ever explained these mysterious occurrences.

Money Through the Mail

A few days before Christmas 1979, a sorter in the main post office of Malmo, Sweden, found an envelope containing a wad of money worth a fortune. There was no name on the envelope and no clue as to where it had come from. A few

That's Peculiar! 15

weeks later, another bundle of money was found in the mail and this continued at regular intervals until February 1981. No one knows who the money belonged to or why it kept turning up in the mail!

Moving with the Mind

Russian housewife Nelya Mikhailova Kulagina has risen to fame because of her extraordinary ability to move things—with her mind. During tests carried out by Soviet scientists, she made a compass needle rotate, caused the yolk to separate from the white of an egg and made a piece of bread move across a table—all without touching them. The scientists have so far been unable to produce a logical explanation.

2 · Unnatural Phenomena

The Haunted Elevator

In 1969, the elevator in a large hotel in Wales began to move by itself. It would rise from the ground floor and go up to the second floor. At first, repairmen thought it must have been an electrical fault, but when the electricity was turned off the lift still moved! It even moved when the cables had been cut!

Lighter than Air

Daniel Dunglas Home was a 19th-century medium. It was said that he could provide evidence of life after death with the appearance of strange lights, ghostly rappings on tables, and by producing ectoplasm, a weird substance thought to come from spirits. It was understandable, therefore, that in August 1852 he should be the guest of honor at a seance at the home of Ward Cheney, a silk manufacturer, in Connecticut. Home was only 19 years old at the time and had produced some remarkable manifestations, but his amazing feat at that house in Connecticut baffled the entire world. For Home, without warning, floated off the ground!

F. L. Burr, editor of the *Hartford Times*, was present when Home levitated. He later wrote: "Suddenly, without any expectation on the part of the company, Home was taken up in the air. I had hold of his hand at the time and I felt his feet—

they were lifted a foot from the floor. He palpitated from head to foot with the contending emotions of joy and fear which choked his utterances. Again and again he was taken from the floor, and the third time he was carried to the ceiling of the apartment, with which his hands and feet came into gentle contact."

Home went on to perform his incredible feat of levitation before many eminent people all over the world.

Bad Habits

A 17th-century monk, Joseph of Copertino, had the distracting habit of lifting off the ground and floating in the air when he became excited. This tended to disturb other monks, so he was asked to pray in the monastery by himself.

The Rain Maker

Could Charles Hatfield make rain? He certainly appeared to be able to do so. In fact, sometimes his rain-making attempts proved too successful!

In 1916, the town council of San Diego hired him to fill a new reservoir. Hatfield went out to the Morena Reservoir in the Laguna Mountains, 60 miles east of San Diego, and set up his equipment. After three days it began to rain!

A few more showers followed during the next weeks and some really heavy downpours came early in January. Hatfield promised even more rain—and it arrived with a vengeance, causing widespread damage and flooding. Delighted with his success, Hatfield went to San Diego to collect his fee. But, the council refused to pay him unless he agreed to pay a bill of $3½ million to cover damages!

In 1922, Hatfield was invited to make rain in Sand Canyon in the California desert. The rain

fell so heavily that the canyon was completely destroyed and a 30-mile length of railway line was washed away. After this episode, and over 500 other successful rain-making attempts, Charles Hatfield decided to retire.

Offered large amounts of money to sell the secret of the chemicals he used to create rain, Hatfield always refused. It was, he said, "too devastating a force to unleash to any one individual, or to a group of bureaucrats who might misuse it." He decided that his secret formula should die with him—and to this day, no one knows how Hatfield managed to make rain.

Wheel from the Sky

One day in 1969, a woman was driving through Palm Springs, California, when an enormous wheel dropped from the sky onto the roof of her car. Naturally, she reported the incident and everyone assumed that the wheel had fallen from a plane. But when authorities checked, they could find no record of any plane losing a wheel that day. It seemed that the wheel had materialized from nowhere!

Falling Frogs

Early one morning in May 1981, the inhabitants of the village of Narplion in southern Greece were surprised to see frogs falling from the sky. Thousands of small African frogs rained down on the village and their croaking drove the villagers to distraction.

Meteorologists in Athens explained the shower of frogs by saying that they must have been sucked up from African marshes by a whirlwind that carried them across the sea to Greece.

This was not the only occasion that Greece experienced a strange rainfall. In 200 A.D. it rained fish for three days!

Queen of the Fire Eaters

Jo Giradelli amazed everyone when she toured England in 1818. She could eat fire, lighted candles, molten metal and boiling oil. She would

take nitric acid into her mouth, hold it there for a while and then spit it out onto iron, which reacted violently to the strong acid. She would dip her fingers into boiling lead, then scoop some out and put it in her mouth.

Scientists at the time thought that she must have some miraculous immunity to heat.

Flight Light

On Eastern Airlines Flight 539 from New York to Washington in March 1962, an airline stewardess and a passenger were dozing in their seats. At 5 o'clock in the morning, their slumber was disturbed suddenly by a crack of lightning that seemed to erupt all through the plane. The noise woke them both and then they received the surprise of their lives. Through the door of the pilot's cabin came a ball of blue-white light. It hovered about two feet above the floor

and then moved down the aisle towards the rear of the plane, where it disappeared.

What had the two of them seen? Some experts say that it was ball lightning but, although there are many recorded instances of this phenomenon, no one seems to know exactly what it is or what causes it.

3 · Monsters You Never Heard Of

Malaysian Mud-man

Many people believe there is a semi-human creature living in the jungles of Malaya. The creature is known as the Mud-man because it often leaves footprints on muddy surfaces. These prints are said to be at least 30 inches long and the creature is about 10 feet tall. So far, no one has ever managed to confront the Mud-man—and perhaps that is just as well!

The Ghost Bird of Lincoln's Inn

A group of men was standing near the lodge of the legal offices at Lincoln's Inn in London on the evening of February 25, 1913, when they heard a terrified scream. They looked up and saw, silhouetted in a window, the figure of a man fighting off an invisible assailant.

They rushed up the stairs to the first floor office but they were too late: Charles Appleby, a young lawyer, lay dead on the floor, covered in blood.

In the months that followed, a number of other tenants occupied the offices, but they all left because of the evil atmosphere of the place. A short while later, another lawyer, John Radlett, was found hanged in the same office where Charles Appleby had been found. There were deep scratches on the inside of his locked door. They looked as if they had been made by the claws of an enormous bird.

When stories began to circulate about the ghost bird that haunted the offices in Lincoln's Inn, two newspaper editors, Sir Max Pemberton and Ralph Blumenfeld, decided to investigate. They locked themselves in the ill-famed room, sprinkled powdered French chalk all over the floor and began their vigil.

The two men spent the evening playing cards, and by midnight they were getting bored with the whole idea. It seemed obvious that nothing was going to happen. They were about to leave, when the locked door swung open. The windows, which had been bolted, opened by themselves, and a harsh wind swept into the room, extinguishing the gaslight.

There was a horrifying beating noise that sounded like the flapping of enormous wings. In the dim light the two men could just about see a large, dark object moving across the room and out through a wall. Then the noise stopped, and the light came on again.

A reporter who had been waiting downstairs heard the commotion and rushed into the room. All three men stared in disbelief at the floor. In the chalk, running from the middle of the room to the corner, were gigantic claw marks!

A few years later the building was demolished and the ghost bird—if that is what it was—was never heard of again.

The Terror of Croglin Hall

For one glorious year, Edward Cranswell was very pleased with his new home, Croglin Hall, in England. But he changed his mind during the summer of 1875.

Amelia, Edward's sister, was unable to sleep one night. She was sitting in her room, gazing out at the garden. Suddenly a strange, dog-like skeleton came bounding across the lawn and began scratching at the window.

Amelia screamed with terror and ran to the door of her room. But she had locked it. In her panic, she dropped the key and couldn't find it in the dark. She could hear her two brothers pounding on her door, but by now, the skeleton had smashed a pane of glass. A bony arm came through the broken pane and began to open the window.

When her brothers eventually managed to open the door, they found Amelia unconscious on the floor. Blood was pouring from terrible wounds on her throat, face and shoulders. Her brother Michael saw the dog-like skeleton running away.

After a long convalescence in Switzerland, Amelia returned to Croglin Hall, in spite of her brothers' misgivings. During her absence there had been other reports in the area of girls being attacked by a strange creature.

It wasn't long before the skeleton appeared again at Croglin. But this time, Amelia's brothers were prepared. They had arranged to sleep near Amelia's room, and they insisted that none of the doors were to be locked. When they heard Amelia's terrified screams, Michael dashed to her room while Edward headed for the front door. They saw the skeleton running towards the churchyard. As it scrambled over the churchyard wall, Edward fired his pistol. The creature staggered for a moment, and then slowly began to make its way to the family vault of the Fishers— the family who had owned Croglin before Edward Cranswell bought it.

The next day, the brothers got some local men to help them break into the vault. Every coffin was shattered and the pieces were strewn across the floor. Only one coffin was intact. They opened it.

Inside was a shrivelled-up dog-like creature. It had a flesh wound in its leg! The villagers agreed that the corpse should be burnt. The terror of Croglin Hall was never seen again.

The Siamese Werewolf

In 1960, Harold M. Young, owner of the Chiengmai Zoo in Thailand, was hunting in the Lahu Mountains when he heard there was a taw— a Siamese werewolf—in a local village. He had heard stories of taws in the past, but this was the closest he had ever come to seeing one.

One night, a scream was heard in one of the village huts. Mr. Young ran to the hut. Inside, he saw a strange wolf-like animal gnawing at the neck of one of the villagers. He fired at the beast, but only managed to graze the side of its body. The creature fled into the jungle.

Next morning, Young took some of the villagers with him to follow the trail of blood left by the wounded beast. They tracked it into the jungle and then, much to their surprise, back into the village once again. The trail of blood led them to a hut where they found a man lying wounded—with a bullet in his side.

Grey Man of Macdhui

At least two people are said to have died of fright when they encountered the "Grey Man of Macdhui." The appearance of this specter on the highest mountain in the Cairngorms in Scotland is often accompanied by the sound of pounding hooves. He sometimes shouts at people in a loud and terrifying voice and chases people who run away from him.

The Great Head of the Marakopa

Mr. John Phillips, a keen angler, hooked more than he bargained for when he went fishing on the Marakopa River in Wellington, New Zealand. At the end of his fishing line was an enormous eel-like creature with a huge head. The creature bit through Phillips' fishing line and then attacked Phillips himself. The terrified angler ran for his life and the creature slipped back into the waters.

There have since been several other sightings of the fearsome creature, which has come to be known as The Great Head of the Marakopa River.

Footprints on the Ice

In 1924 James Rennie and a French Canadian trapper were out hunting when they noticed strange footprints on a frozen lake. The trapper warned Rennie of impending danger: he was convinced that the footprints belonged to the Wyndygo, a monster said to live in the Himalayan Mountains.

Rennie paid no attention to the trapper's warnings and began to cross the frozen lake. He was about half a mile from shore when new footprints began to appear. Something invisible seemed to be moving towards Rennie over the frozen lake. The tracks were getting closer and closer, but there was not a creature in sight!

Soon the footprints reached Rennie. Suddenly, he was hit in the face by a cold splash of water. Then the tracks continued their strange journey across the lake.

4 · Isn't *That* a Coincidence?

Description of Disaster

"**T**he world's largest liner, on her maiden voyage, hits an iceberg and sinks. Most of the passengers are drowned because there are not enough lifeboats . . ."

This may sound like a description of the sinking of the *Titanic* in 1912, but it is, in fact, the plot from a novel by Morgan Robertson, written in 1898. The name of the ship in the book is the *Titan*!

On April 14, 1912, the *Titanic* hit an iceberg and sank. Over 1,500 passengers and crew were drowned.

Predicting the Future

Nostradamus was a 16th-century Frenchman who could apparently predict the future. In his writings, he foresaw the Great Fire of London in 1666, the rise of Hitler, the rise of General Franco in Spain in the 1930s, and World War II.

As well as foreseeing these major historic events, he predicted the work of scientist Louis Pasteur, who developed the process for pasteurizing milk, and the abdication of King Edward VIII from the British throne.

Nostradamus even predicted his own death in 1566. Before he died, he went to an engraver and asked him to engrave a date on a small metal plate, and instructed that it should be placed in his coffin. In 1700 it was decided to move the coffin from the grave, where it had lain for 134 years, to a more prominent spot. Before it was lowered into the earth, the coffin was opened. Inside, the metal plate bore the date 1700.

The Amazing Mother Shipton

f her friends insulted her, Ursula Southill would toss them in the air by means of an invisible orce. It was a technique she probably inherited rom her mother, Agatha, who was reputed to be a vitch.

Ursula, who was born in July 1488, married To-bias Shipton when she was 24 and it was as Mother Shipton that she became famous. She was known best for her powers of prediction, and is redited with foreseeing the invention of the ra-dio, the automobile and the airplane. She also pre-dicted two world wars, at least 350 years before they happened!

Umberto's Double

In July 1900, King Umberto I of Italy was eating at a restaurant, when someone noticed that the restaurant owner bore a strong resemblance to him. The coincidence did not end there. It turned

out that the restaurateur's name was also Umberto. Both men had been born in Turin on the same day. Both had wives called Margherita, and each had a son called Vittorio. On the day of the king's coronation the other man had opened his restaurant.

The day after the meeting, the king attended a game at the sports stadium and he invited the restaurateur to go along as his guest. When he got to the stadium, he was shocked to hear that the restaurateur had been shot that morning. Later that day, King Umberto was, himself, assassinated!

Royal Connections

Just like the restaurant owner and King Umberto I, ironmonger Samuel Hemming looked like King George III. The two men were also born on the same day, June 4, 1738. And, in the same ways, the coincidence continued. Both men were married on September 8, 1761, and both had the

same number of children of the same sex. On the day George III ascended the throne, Hemming opened his shop. They both became ill on the same day and they both died on the same day!

Crossword of Coincidence

On May 22, 1944, during World War II, one of the clues in the crossword puzzle in the *Daily Telegraph*, a British newspaper, led to a remarkable spy hunt. The clue was "One of the US,"

and the correct answer was "Utah." A few days later, the answer to another crossword clue in the same newspaper was "Omaha." A few days after this, another answer was "Mulberry."

It was not long before M15, the British security service, began to take an interest, for "Utah," "Omaha" and "Mulberry" were all code names for the Allied invasion of France, Operation Overlord. A few days later, the word "Neptune" appeared in the crossword. That convinced M15 that a spy

was sending secret messages to the enemy, because "Neptune" was the code word for naval operations during the D-Day landings.

M15 immediately visited Leonard Dawe, who compiled the crosswords for the *Daily Telegraph*. But, far from being a German spy, he was a schoolmaster from Surrey. The secret code words had appeared in the crosswords by pure coincidence, but how so many of them could appear in such quick succession and at such a sensitive time is quite a mystery!

Presidential Perplexer

Remarkable similarities have been found between presidents Abraham Lincoln and John F. Kennedy.

Both men were assassinated. Lincoln's assassin, John Wilkes Booth, was born in 1839; Kennedy's killer, Lee Harvey Oswald, was born in 1939. Both presidents were shot in the head from behind on a Friday, and in the presence of their wives. Lincoln's secretary, whose name was Ken-

nedy, advised him not to go to the theatre where he was assassinated; Kennedy's secretary, whose name was Lincoln, advised him not to go to Dallas, where he was assassinated.

To cap it all off, Abraham Lincoln was elected in 1860 and John F. Kennedy came to office in 1960!

Seeing Beyond the Horizon

In the 18th century, French scientist Bottineau claimed he could "see" beyond the horizon by observing the effect approaching ships had on the atmosphere. Bottineau called his new science *nauscopy*. Between 1778 and 1782, he successfully predicted the arrival at the Île de France (now Mauritius) of 575 ships, as long as four days before they docked.

Bottineau's predictions continued to be extremely accurate, and in 1784 he approached the French government, offering his services. The French ministers were suspicious and called Bottineau a crank. He died in 1789, and the secret of nauscopy died with him.

The Hotel Dresser Switch

U.S. journalist Irv Kupcinet, went to London in 1953 to cover the coronation of Queen Elizabeth II. He was very surprised when, on his arrival at the hotel, he opened a drawer in his room. Inside the drawer were several items belonging to a friend of his, basketball player Harry Hannin.

He forgot about it until a few days later, when Hannin wrote him from Paris. Apparently, Hannin had found one of Kupcinet's ties in his hotel room in Paris!

5 · Ghost to the Rescue!

Cast the Lead, Sir!

In the early years of this century, a sailor on the ship HMS *Society* was drowned. A few nights later the captain was woken up by the sailor's ghost. "Cast the lead, sir!" said the apparition. Then it vanished.

When the captain did as he had been instructed, he found that his ship was off course and sailing in only 36 feet of water! The ghost's warning had prevented the ship from running aground.

Guardian of the Bomber

In 1977, the Lincoln bomber RF398 was taken to the RAF Aerospace Museum hangar for repairs. It was not long before the men working on the plane began seeing a mysterious airman. He was always either in the hangar or standing on the wing of the plane, dressed in a leather jacket and white polo-necked sweater—a style popular with early aviators. They knew that he wasn't a member of the crew or the administration and no one ever was able to get close enough to speak with him.

After a while, the men came to the conclusion that the airman was a phantom who was protecting both the plane and the men who were working on it. One engineer fell backwards from the wing 15 feet onto the concrete floor—but was completely uninjured. Another man walked into the sharp edge of a propeller and was also unhurt. Strange whistling was heard, and on a cold day, when there were icicles hanging from the roof, it was so cosy inside the plane that the men didn't even have to wear coats.

The repairmen never discovered who their strange protector had been, but they were glad he was there, all the same.

The Monk Who Prevented a Suicide

On a night in 1917, during World War I, General Luigi Cadorna, chief of the Italian General Staff, sat in his tent mourning the defeat of his troops by the enemy. It seemed to him the only thing to do was to kill himself. He had raised a loaded pistol to his head when, suddenly, a monk appeared in the tent. "Don't be so foolish," said the monk, and then he vanished.

The general did not kill himself that night. Several years later, he was visiting the Church of San Giovanni Rotondo at Foggia in Italy, when he saw the same monk who had visited him in his tent. He was a peasant priest named Padre Pio. When he saw the general, the monk said, "You had a lucky escape, my friend."

Although General Cadorna had seen him in his tent in 1917, he learned that Padre Pio had never left the monastery during the war.

Ghostly Life Saver

During the summer of 1965, Peter and Irene Nierman moored their barge near Tertogenbosch in Holland. One day, while Peter was ashore, their five-year-old son Willem fell into the water. Irene screamed, but there was nothing she could do to save the boy. She was expecting another child, and her husband was out of earshot. Some workmen heard her cries, but they were too far away to prevent the boy from drowning in the fast-flowing waters. Then suddenly a dark-haired man appeared at the water's edge. Within seconds he was in the water alongside the boy, cradling him in his arms.

Although she had been watching him since he first appeared, Irene had not actually seen the man jump into the water. But she did not think about that at the time, because she was so relieved to have her son back safe and sound. She ran ashore to thank the stranger, but by the time she reached her son, the man was already walking away towards a nearby warehouse. When she looked again, he had disappeared. By now the dock workers, who had heard her cries, were on the scene and they asked Irene why she was looking at the warehouses. When she described the person who had rescued Willem, the men sud-

denly became very quiet and asked no further questions about the incident.

The next day Peter Nierman tried to find Willem's rescuer so that he could thank him. After many hours of searching, he discovered that the man who had saved his son's life was well known in the area. He was Johan Udink, a dock worker who had drowned at that very spot—10 years before.

Tightrope Rescue

Pierre Hurette was determined that he would perform his tightrope act at the Olympiadrome in Paris as planned. His doctors had advised him against it. He had been in the hospital for four weeks following an accident on the high wire in which his partner had been killed. Hurette's ribs were encased in tape and his arm

was still heavily bandaged, but he was intent on following the old show business tradition—"the show must go on".

Because of his injuries, Hurette found the climb to the high wire extremely difficult, but he was determined to succeed. Walking across the wire, each step was more painful than the last. He faltered when he reached the halfway point. It was clear that the strain had proved too much and he was going to fall, when suddenly another figure appeared on the high wire. He steadied Hurette and then walked to the end of the wire, where a

rope was hanging. He brought the rope back to Hurette, who grasped it in desperation. With the rope Hurette was able to reach the end of the wire and then climb down to safety. When he looked up again, the figure had vanished.

Hurette recognized the man who saved his life on the high wire that summer day. And he wasn't

the only one. Many others recognized him as Paul de Champ, who had been Hurette's partner until the accident four weeks previously in which he had been killed. The audience packed into the Olympiadrome had witnessed the amazing spectacle of a ghost saving a human life.

6 · Poltergeist!

Investigations in Enfield

In 1977 psychical experts, reporters and also the police were invited to a house in Enfield, England, to investigate strange happenings. Mrs. Peggy Hodgson and her four children were being pestered by a poltergeist and they wanted to put an end to their problems.

The investigators reported that furniture moved around the house by itself and that toy bricks flew about the rooms. A photographer from the *Daily Mirror* was hit on the forehead by a flying brick.

There were also mysterious rapping noises. Investigators were unable to come up with any logical explanation for the phenomenon.

Finally, psychical researcher Maurice Grosse managed to communicate with the unwanted "house guest." The poltergeist was thought to be the ghost of Bill Hobbs, who had died in the house many years previously. Hobbs had apparently come back from Durant's Park graveyard to see his family and was angry when he found that they no longer lived there.

The Rosenheim Phenomena

In November 1967 strange things began to happen in an attorney's office in Rosenheim, Germany. Fluorescent light tubes began unscrewing themselves from their sockets. Four telephones rang at the same time. Liquid poured out of the photocopier. The electric company was called in, but engineers could find nothing wrong. The fluorescent tubes were replaced by ordinary light

bulbs. They burst. Drawers in filing cabinets opened and closed by themselves. A heavy cabinet moved away from the wall and a picture rotated on its hook!

Professor Hans Bender, director of the Institute for the Frontiers of Psychology, was called in to investigate. He found that these weird happenings occurred only in the presence of a young girl who worked in the office. However, the girl herself played no conscious part in causing the strange events.

Water, Water, Everywhere

In Stuhlingen, West Germany, Elsa Arndt found a small puddle of water on her dining room floor. She assumed that one of her daughters had spilled the water accidentally and mopped it up carelessly. But then she found a pool of water on her bed and some more on the bathroom floor.

Elsa believed that her daughters were playing a

trick on her, until water began gushing from the walls! Her husband, Irvin, called in a plumber who could find nothing wrong with the plumbing.

When, one day, blobs of water actually appeared in mid-air, the Arndt family decided to approach Hans Bender, who was well known in Germany for his psychic investigations. Bender first turned off the water supply to the house at the main pipe, but still the water came. In one test, Bender had a bedroom completely sealed up, even going so far as to block the keyhole, but when he reopened the room there was a pool of water on the floor.

After three weeks, with water appearing in the house up to 60 times each day, the water suddenly stopped coming. Hans Bender came to the conclusion that the water had been caused by a poltergeist that was trying to contact twelve-year-old Sabine Arndt, Elsa's daughter.

The Poltergeist of Barking Creek

John Willis and his wife Rosemary were watching television one evening at their home in Essex, England, when suddenly they heard the sound of loud crashing and banging coming from their children's room. The couple rushed upstairs to find out what was wrong. As they entered the bedroom, an ornament crashed against the wall, narrowly missing Rosemary's head. The room seemed alive with activity. Bedding and toys were flying around the room. Cowering together in the corner were their children, ten-year-old Terry and seven-year-old Sandra, terrified out of their wits.

The Willises bundled their two children out of the room, and slammed the bedroom door shut. All four stood on the landing shaking with fear and unable to understand what strange phenomenon could be responsible for what they had witnessed in the room.

From July to September 1952, the Willis family had to endure a continuous barrage of these happenings in their house. Objects flew around rooms. A kitchen table split in half as the family looked on. An iron poker bent in half. The sitting-room curtains were ripped to shreds by unseen hands.

Although no one in the house was ever hurt by

the poltergeist, Norman Horridge, an expert on the paranormal, was convinced that a strange and evil force existed in the house. He persuaded the Willis family to agree to an exorcism.

The exorcism was carried out in September 1952. Doors blew open and banged to and fro, as if the poltergeist was angry at being banished. But, finally the house went quiet—the poltergeist had departed forever.

Shell Shock

George Newman was the groundskeeper on Lord Portman's estate in Dorset, England. In December 1894, the residents began telling him stories of strange manifestations in the area. Objects were floating in the air and being hurled around the rooms. Soon, Newman himself began to see strange things. Much to his surprise, he saw a toy whistle that floated in the air and then banged itself against a window.

The groundskeeper was intrigued and he decided to keep watch to see if anything else happened. Later he described this scene: "I saw, coming from behind the door, a quantity of little shells," he wrote. "They came round the door at a

height of about five feet, one at a time, at intervals varying from half a minute to a minute. They came very slowly and when they hit me I could hardly feel them. With the shells, two thimbles came so slowly that in the ordinary way they would have dropped long before they reached me. Both thimbles struck my hat. Some missed my head and went down slanting-wise (not as if they were dropped). Those that struck me fell straight down."

A number of so-called "explanations" were offered, but no one knows exactly what caused these objects to float as Newman swears they did.

7 · Tricks in Time

Time of Death

Pope Paul VI was presented with an alarm clock in 1923. It served him faithfully for 55 years, waking him promptly at six o'clock every morning. On Sunday, August 6, 1978, the alarm clock rang, apparently of its own accord, at 9:40 p.m.—the very moment that the Pope died.

A Step Backwards

Dr. E. G. Moon had been visiting a patient in Kent, England. He stepped out of the house only to find that his car was missing—and so was the hedge and the road! The scenery was completely different than it had been when he had entered the house a short while earlier. He was now looking at a muddy track. A young man in old-fashioned clothes was walking by.

Puzzled, Dr. Moon turned to go back into the house—and then glanced over his shoulder for another look. Everything was back to normal! Later he did a little research on what he had witnessed. The scene, as he had viewed it, looked exactly the way it would have looked 100 years earlier! It seems that, for a few seconds, he had been transported back in time.

The Strange Disappearance of Lucy Lightfoot

On the morning of June 13, 1831, a young girl named Lucy Lightfoot entered St. Olave's church on the Isle of Wight. She had gone to look at a statue of Edward Estur, a 14th-century crusader knight, who died at Gatcombe and was buried nearby.

Later that day, a local farmer spotted Lucy's horse outside the church. Inside the church, a jeweled dagger had been torn from the statue and was lying on the ground. A fine jewel from the dagger was missing and so was Lucy.

Lucy was never heard of again. Thirty-five years later, the minister Samuel Trelawney found some documents relating to the Crusades. He discovered that when Edward Estur left for the Middle East in 1363, he had taken with him a girl from the Isle of Wight. Her name was Lucy Lightfoot!

Accident in Time

In the early 1960s in Kyle of Lochalsh, Scotland, a car plunged into the sea and its occupants were drowned. The car was identical to a phantom car that had been sighted regularly in the region for over 20 years. After this accident, the ghost vehicle was never seen again.

The Headless Cyclist

As he walked toward the Fox and Hounds Inn near Northampton one winter's day in 1940, George Dobbs saw a car coming along the snow-covered road. Approaching the car from the opposite direction was a man on a bicycle. George Dobbs blinked his eyes several times—the man appeared to have no head.

The driver of the car did not seem to see the cyclist, but continued to head straight for him.

Within seconds the car had passed. George was convinced that the cyclist must have been hit, and he ran over to help. But the cyclist had vanished.

When he arrived at the inn, Dobbs told his friends about his strange experience. Then one of them, the local gravedigger, said, "There was an accident at that spot 25 years ago. A cyclist was knocked off his bike in deep snow—the accident severed his head."

Shipwreck on Goodwin Sands

Soon after the start of World War II, a guard on watch on the East Goodwin lightship in southern England saw an old-fashioned paddle steamer run aground on the treacherous Goodwin sandbars. The guard called the Ramsgate lifeboat station, and a lifesaving crew sped to the scene. The whole area was searched, but there was no sign of any wreckage or casualties. When the guard re-

lated how the shipwreck occurred, old-timers realized that he was describing exactly the sinking of the SS *Violet*—a steamer that had gone down many years before!

Message in a Bottle

In 1882 one of the crew of the Brazilian gunboat *Araguary* fished a bottle out of the sea. In it was a message: "Aboard the schooner *Sea Hero*. The crew has mutinied, killing the captain and flinging the first mate overboard. I am the second mate and have been spared to navigate the ship. They are forcing me to head for the Amazon River, 28° long. 22° lat. making 2½ knots. Rush help."

The letter was undated, but since they were not far from the spot, the captain of the *Araguary* decided to investigate. When they reached the position given, they spotted the *Sea Hero*. Firing a warning shot, the gunboat captain ordered the vessel to come alongside. A boarding party went aboard the *Sea Hero*, arrested the mutineers and rescued the second mate.

The second mate was pleased to be rescued, but he could not understand how the gunboat captain knew of the mutiny. The captain explained that they had found the bottle, but the mate denied having sent any message.

At the court trial the mystery deepened. The *Sea Hero* had been named after a novel written 16 years earlier by John Parminton. As a publicity stunt, the author had put 5,000 bottles, with phony messages in them, into the sea. It was one of these that the *Araguary* picked up—16 years later!

8 · Getting Away with Murder

Footprint in Blood

On Christmas Eve, 1684, William Blatt's family was at home in Yorkshire, England, when they saw William walking up the staircase towards the main bedroom. They were surprised, because William Blatt was supposed to be in London at the time.

Blatt's wife and children ran after him, but when they got to the top of the staircase, there was no one there. All that could be seen was a single footprint on the floor—it was of fresh blood! William Blatt had, in fact, been cruelly murdered that very evening—in London.

The Haunted Bolero

For the play, *The Queen Came By*, at the Duke of York Theatre in London, actress Thora Hird had to wear a long dress topped with an embroidered velvet bolero jacket. Whenever she wore it, however, she experienced a choking sensation. Her understudy underwent the same sensation when she wore it, as did the stage manager and the director's wife.

The jacket proved to be quite a problem. Three mediums were called in, but to no avail. Three members of the cast were asked to try the jacket on, and two of them felt as if they were being choked by it, too.

After some research into the history of the jacket, a Victorian original, it was discovered that the owner had been throttled to death by her lover while wearing it. She had haunted the garment ever since.

The Garden Ghost

In 1938, soon after the Carr family moved into a vicarage in Wiltshire, England, a girl in white began making regular appearances. Ten-year-old Frances and seven-year-old Janet were the first to see her. They told their mother about the girl who would come close to them but run away when they spoke to her.

Mrs. Carr thought her daughters were imagining things—until she saw the girl herself. One day, while sitting in the garden with a friend, Mrs. Carr heard the gate open. A little girl, wearing a white dress and carrying a small parcel, walked

up the path and went into the house. A few minutes later, she came out again and walked away. When the housekeeper brought out a tray of tea, Mrs. Carr asked about the visitor, but the housekeeper knew nothing about her. None of the other servants had seen her either.

The girl in white was seen frequently after that. Most often she was on her own, but several times she was seen with an old man. She was always crying when the man was with her.

The Carr family eventually left the vicarage, and after World War II the building was vacant for a few years. It was finally pulled down in 1953. During the demolition, workmen found a closet that had been bricked up. Beneath the floorboards of the closet they found the skeleton of a young girl and what remained of a white dress.

Death in Bed

On the night of May 31, 1810, the Duke of Cumberland had just returned from a visit to the opera, when his valet, Sellis, tried to kill him. The attempt was unsuccessful, and later that night Sellis committed suicide.

That, at least, was the duke's version of events on that fateful night. However, it was not long before rumors began to circulate that Sellis had, in fact, been blackmailing the Duke of Cumberland and that the duke had actually murdered his valet.

It seems that this rumor may well have been the truth, and the Duke of Cumberland's version of events a lie. Because, after that night, the valet's ghost was seen several times—sitting up in his bed with his throat cut!

Killer Bus

In the spring of 1933 a man was driving along St. Mark's Road in London, when he saw a double-decker bus careening towards him. It was too late to avoid a collision—the bus had appeared from nowhere and all the car driver could do was

to slam on his brakes and await the impact. But nothing happened. When the driver opened his eyes, the bus was nowhere in sight!

That was not the first time the mysterious bus was sighted. On one occasion, a driver swerved to avoid a bus that was out of control and actually crashed his car into one of the houses on the street. But when he turned back to look again, the bus had disappeared.

Several other sightings of the ghost bus were reported and a number of accidents occurred on the same street. Luckily, none of the drivers were seriously injured—until Monday, June 11, 1933, when two cars crashed head-on, killing one of the drivers. After this fatal accident, the ghost bus disappeared forever—perhaps satisfied that it had claimed at least one victim.

Revenge of the Skulls

When Myles Phillipson, a government official, moved into his new house, Calgarth Hall in northern England, he invited his friends to a housewarming. The party was in full swing when, suddenly, the guests heard Phillipson's wife

scream. The found her on the staircase staring at two grinning skulls.

Phillipson threw the skulls out of the house, but during the night they reappeared on the staircase. In the days that followed, Phillipson tried every means to get rid of the skulls, but no matter what he did they always returned.

News of the menacing skulls spread, and soon Phillipson found that his business was in financial trouble. Over the next few months, his wealth steadily diminished until he was left virtually penniless. Finally, Phillipson died, a broken man.

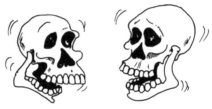

It turned out that the two skulls were those of a man and his wife who had previously owned Calgarth Hall. Phillipson had wanted to own the property so much that he had had them executed for a crime they had not committed.

On the night of Phillipson's death, the skulls could be heard laughing throughout the house. They had their revenge at last.

9 · Traveling with Ghosts

Follow the Moving Light. . . .

Two English policemen, Clifford Waycott and Roger Wiley, could hardly believe their eyes early one morning in October 1967. Hovering above their car was a ball of bright light. When the light began to move away from them, they followed it in their car but were unable to catch it. Then another light, shaped like a cross, joined the first. The two lights eventually disappeared, leaving the policemen absolutely baffled.

The Girl Who Wasn't There

On July 13, 1974, Maurice Goodenough was driving up Bluebell Hill in Kent, England, when suddenly a young girl appeared in his headlights. He hit the brakes as hard as he could, but he was not quick enough and the car hit the girl. Maurice jumped out of the car and ran over to where she was lying. She had serious head injuries, but he couldn't leave her in the middle of the road. He carried her to the roadside, covered her with a blanket, and drove to the nearest police station for help.

The police rushed to the scene of the accident, but when they arrived all they found was the blanket. The girl had vanished. Tracker dogs were used to find her, but without success.

Later, Maurice discovered that other drivers had seen the girl on other occasions. Some had even given her a ride, but each time she had vanished. Apparently, two girls had been killed at that spot in 1967. Perhaps one of them had come back as a ghost.

The Phantom Hitchhiker

One evening, truck driver Harold Unsworth stopped to pick up a hitchhiker who asked for a ride to Old Beam Bridge. As they drove along, the hitchhiker talked, in gory detail, of all the accidents that had happened at the bridge.

A few months later, Unsworth was driving along the same strip of road when he saw the same hitchhiker. Once again, he gave the hitchhiker a ride to Old Beam Bridge, and once again the hitchhiker spoke about the accidents that had happened there. When they arrived at the bridge, the hitchhiker got out, but asked Unsworth to wait a few moments while he collected his belongings. The truck driver waited for 20 minutes, but the hitchhiker did not return, so he decided to drive on without him.

To Unsworth's amazement, three miles further on, there in the road stood the hitchhiker. Suddenly, he jumped in front of the truck. Unsworth

slammed on the brakes, but although it was far too late to avoid hitting the man, he felt no impact. Unsworth looked in his rear view mirror and saw the hitchhiker, seemingly unharmed, waving his fist furiously at the truck. Suddenly, the hitchhiker vanished.

Unsworth could come up with only one explanation—the man had to be a ghost. Perhaps he was a victim of one of the accidents he described so vividly.

That Explains It!

Each Christmas, at Penryn in Cornwall, England, a phantom carriage, drawn by headless horses, is said to appear. But you won't find any eyewitnesses. Everyone who has seen the specter, they say, has vanished from the face of the earth within a few hours.

Grateful to Drivers

The ghost of Nance is often seen by truck drivers traveling to York in northern England. She runs alongside the moving trucks and if there is any danger ahead, she slows them down to warn them.

Nance was an 18th-century farmer's daughter who left her fiancé to marry a highwayman. But the highwayman was already married. He deserted Nance, leaving her pregnant and penniless. Nance's ex-fiancé, a stagecoach driver, found her several months later, standing on the York road with her baby. He took her home to care for her, but both she and the baby died. Because of this driver's kindness, Nance's ghost has been helping all kinds of drivers ever since.

The Vanishing Hitchhiker

Many people have stopped to give rides to a hitchhiker at Frome, Somerset, in the west

of England. The hitchhiker, who always wears a checked sports jacket, asks to be driven to Nunney Catch—but by the time they get there he has disappeared!

Submarine Spook

On January 21, 1918, three officers were standing on the bridge of the German submarine *U-65* when they spotted a man standing near the bow. Where he had come from they could not imagine for the submarine had only just surfaced. The officers shouted to the man, but when he turned to look up at the bridge, they received a shock: glaring at them was Lieutenant Forster, who had been killed a few months before! The ghost stared at the men for a minute or so, then vanished as suddenly as he had appeared.

Ghost Ship of Diamond Shoals

The cargo schooner *Carroll Deering* was found aground on Diamond Shoals, North Carolina, on January 30th, 1921. Her sails were still set but there was no one on board, except for two cats. A meal was out on the table, but it had not been touched. The vessel had been sighted the previous day and had appeared quite normal. There was no clue as to what had happened to the crew. Even today people in the area talk about the "ghost" ship of Diamond Shoals.

Ghosts of the Goodwins

The Goodwin Sands, off the Kent coast, are said to be haunted by many ships that have floundered on these treacherous sandbars. The three-masted schooner, *Lady Lovibond*, was lost with all hands in 1748, but a ghost of the vessel has been seen at 50-year intervals ever since. If

the apparition keeps to this strange and inexplicable schedule, she will make her next ghostly appearance in 1998. But the *Lady Lovibond* is only one of several shipwrecked vessels that haunt this area. Many other sightings will probably be reported before the *Lady Lovibond* makes her next scheduled appearance.

The Flying Dutchman

*T*he *Flying Dutchman* is the most famous ghost ship in the world. It is usually seen around the Cape of Good Hope in South Africa, and is said to be the ghost of a Dutch ship lost in a storm during the 16th century.

There have been many recorded sightings of the *Dutchman*, but the most impressive one was made by Prince George (later George V) and his brother, Prince Albert, in July 1881. The princes described an apparition they saw as "a strange red light as of a phantom ship all aglow, in the midst of which light the mast, spars and sails of a brig 200 yards distant stood out in strong relief."

Spirits in the Air

Captain Robert Loft and Second Officer Don Repo died when their Eastern Airlines L-1011 TriStar crashed in Florida on December 29th, 1972, but their ghosts were seen for quite some time afterwards. The first sighting was made by one of the airline's vice-presidents. He had just turned to speak with a uniformed pilot on a flight to San Francisco when he suddenly realized he was talking to Captain Loft. The figure then vanished.

In February 1974, on a flight to Mexico City, a stewardess saw Don Repo. She mentioned this to the flight engineer who said that he, too, had seen him. He said Repo had warned him to watch out for fire on the plane. Sure enough, when the plane took off from Mexico City, one of the engines burst into flames. Fortunately, the fire was put out quickly.

The two men were seen on several other flights during 1974 but have not been seen since.

Mystery in the Museum

The wartime B-29 bomber, *Raz'n Hell*, in California's Castle Air Force Museum, did not have any bulbs or batteries. No wonder the museum staff got a shock when the landing lights came on one day.

That was not the only strange occurrence on the plane. Locked doors swung open of their own accord and a shadowy shape was seen in the cockpit. Some of the museum staff were convinced that the craft was being haunted by the dead crew.

10 · Ghostly Hands

The Severed Hand

While he was visiting Luxor, Egypt in 1890, Count Luis Hamon was asked to visit a prominent Arab sheik. Hamon was well known as a psychic healer, and he had been asked to cure the sheik of malaria. This he did, and the grateful sheik gave him an unusual gift in return. It was the mummified hand of an ancient Egyptian princess.

The princess's hand had been cut off by her father, King Akhnaton, in an argument. Hamon offered the hand to various museums, but no one

was willing to accept it, so it was eventually locked away in the safe in Hamon's London home. It remained there for over 30 years, until, one day in 1922, Count Hamon's wife opened the safe to find that the hand was no longer shrivelled. Its appearance had changed to that of a healthy-looking living hand.

The Countess insisted that the hand be disposed of immediately, and her husband agreed. It was decided that the hand should be given a proper funeral, out of respect for the dead princess. This was arranged for the night of October 31. During the funeral service, Count Hamon laid the hand in the fireplace and then read a passage from the *Egyptian Book of the Dead.* Suddenly, there was a clap of thunder and a blast of wind blew open the door to the sitting room.

In the doorway was the figure of a woman dressed in the traditional clothes of an Egyptian princess. Her right arm had been severed. The

figure approached the fireplace, bent over towards the hand and then vanished.

When the Count and Countess recovered sufficiently from their fright, they searched the fireplace. The hand had vanished, and it was never seen again.

The Moving Coffins

The Walrond family tomb was built from rock at Christ Church, Barbados. Only one member of the family, Mrs. Thomasina Goddard, was actually buried in the tomb. In 1808, a year after Mrs. Goddard's death, the Walronds sold the tomb. The Chase family bought it to bury one of their daughters. A second daughter was buried in the tomb in 1812.

Later that year Thomas Chase died. When the large marble door of the tomb was opened for the entombment of Mr. Chase's coffin, it was found that the coffins of his two daughters were standing on end, upside down.

In 1816 another member of the Chase family was being buried in the tomb when, once again, it was noticed that the Chase coffins had been disturbed. As before, there was no sign that anyone had entered the tomb.

Two months later there was another death in the

family and when the tomb, which had been sealed, was opened, all four Chase coffins had been moved. Only the coffin of Mrs. Goddard remained in its rightful place.

In 1819, Lord Combermere, the Governor of Barbados, ordered the tomb to be properly sealed. A year later, noises were heard coming from the tomb. The Governor had it opened up—again. And again, the Chase coffins were scattered about, while the coffin of Mrs. Goddard remained untouched.

It seems that the spirit of Mrs. Goddard was trying to tell the Chase family that they were unwelcome guests in the Walrond family tomb, even if she was the only one there!

Getting Out of Hand

For almost 70 years, a pair of ghostly hands have been scaring people traveling across the Devon moors. In the 1920s, the phantom hands overturned pony carts, and more recently, people have had the steering wheels of their cars plucked from their grasp. A local resident, Florence Warwick, actually saw the hands clambering across the windshield of her car. They disappeared when she screamed in terror.

Eyeless Sight

Indian performer Kuda Bux toured the world giving demonstrations of his eyeless sight. Even with a thick blindfold over his eyes, he was still able to identify any object placed before him. Scientists and doctors tested him by placing lumps of dough on his eyes. These were covered with metal foil, then a wool bandage and, finally, by several layers of gauze. Even so, Bux could read books, ride a bicycle and do many other things, as if he could see perfectly. In spite of extensive scientific investigations of his powers, no one was able to prove that any trickery was involved.

Invisible Barrier

As she tried to back into a parking space in Durham, England, in December 1975, Mrs. Dilys Cant was stopped by an invisible barrier. Three times she tried to get into the parking space, but each time an invisible wall blocked the car.

Mrs. Cant telephoned her daughter-in-law and told her about the strange occurrence, and her daughter-in-law drove to the parking lot to meet her. When she got there she found another baffled motorist. He, too, had tried to park and been stopped by an invisible wall.

Later the barrier, or whatever it was, disappeared. No one could give any explanation for this strange occurrence.

11 · Dreams

The Pot of Gold

John Chapman, who lived in the town of Swaffham, in England, was a poor peddler. One day he had a strange dream in which he was told that he would meet a man on London Bridge who would bring him good luck.

John Chapman walked 100 miles to London. For three days and three nights he waited on London Bridge, but no one approached him.

Eventually, he decided he was silly to have believed in his dream. He was about to go back home to Swaffham, when a shopkeeper came up to him and asked why he had been standing there for three days. Chapman recounted his strange dream.

The shopkeeper laughed at Chapman's story. "Why," he said, "if I paid any attention to my dreams, I'd be in the town of Swaffham right now. For I dreamed that a man there by the name of John Chapman has a pot of gold buried in his garden."

Chapman rushed back home and dug at the spot indicated in the shopkeeper's dream—and sure enough, he found a pot full of gold!

Chapman was so grateful he donated some of his find to the local church. It built the north aisle of the Swaffham church of Saints Peter and Paul.

Dream of Death

One night in 1806, Countess Toutschkoff dreamed she was at an inn in a strange town. In the course of the dream, her father walked into the room with her young son and told her that her husband had been killed at a place called Borodino. She dreamed the same dream on two other occasions and she told her husband, a

general in the Russian army, about it. They looked at several maps, but nowhere could they find a place called Borodino.

On September 7, 1812, Count Toutschkoff was with the Russian army, fighting the French, about 70 miles west of Moscow. Countess Toutschkoff and her family were staying at an inn a few miles away. The next day her father entered the room with her son. "He has been killed in action," he said, referring to her husband. The name of the village where the battle had been fought was Borodino.

Assassinated in a Dream

On May 3, 1812, John Williams of Redruth, England, dreamed that he visited the House of Commons in London where he saw a man shot to death by an assassin who was wearing a dark green coat with shiny brass buttons. When, in the dream, he asked the name of the dead man, he

was told it was Spencer Perceval, who was, at the time, Prime Minister.

The dream so upset Williams that, the following day, he told his wife and all his friends about it. He felt that he should travel to London to warn the Prime Minister, but his friends laughed and told him not to be so silly.

On May 11, Spencer Perceval was shot in the lobby of the House of Commons. His assassin wore a green coat with shiny brass buttons.

Where There's a Will

Nine days after his father's death in May 1948, Leslie Freedman had a strange dream. In the dream he saw his father, Leonard, sitting at his office desk. His father turned towards him and said, "I want you to call the family together at seven o'clock on Saturday."

Leslie Freedman was not sure what to do about his dream, but he called the family together as requested—although he didn't dare tell anyone why!

By 6:50 p.m. the entire family had arrived and they sat in the dining room next to the library, waiting for Leslie Freedman to explain why he had called the meeting.

Suddenly, the whole family found themselves staring through the open door into the library.

There, looking at some books, was the ghost of Leonard Freedman. The specter pointed to one of the books and then vanished.

It was Leslie's brother, Arthur, who moved first. He went into the library and took out the book the phantom had pointed to. It was *A History of Lighthouses on the Irish Coast.*

Arthur flipped through the pages in curious amazement. Inside the front cover was Leonard Freedman's last will and testament—a document that the family had been searching for ever since his death.

The Fatal Hour

In 1779 Lord Thomas Lyttleton dreamed that he was to die in three days' time at midnight. It upset him so much that the following morning he

told all his friends. They tried to reassure him that everything would be all right, but he could not get the dream out of his mind. During the following days he suffered bouts of extreme depression as the fatal hour neared.

On the third evening, he invited some guests to dinner in an attempt to forget about the dream. As midnight approached he became more and more depressed. Eventually, he could take no more, and retired to his bedroom to await death.

He lay on his bed and watched the clock tick away his final seconds. As the clock struck midnight, Lord Lyttleton wondered how he was to

die—but nothing happened! A few minutes later one of his guests looked into the room to see how he was and was surprised to find him in high spirits. "I've beaten death," cried Lyttleton. "I'll be down to join you all shortly."

But Lyttleton didn't appear. When the butler entered the room a little later, he found his lordship lying on the bed gasping for breath. The butler rushed downstairs for help, but it was too late. Lord Lyttleton was dead. "Well," said one of the guests, looking at the bedroom clock, "his dream was almost right, but the time was slightly wrong. It's now half past twelve."

"No, sir, it is not," said the butler. "Because his lordship was so worried, I took the liberty of altering all the household clocks earlier today." The dream was true—Lyttleton had died on the stroke of midnight.

12 · Ghostly Apparitions

The Agreement

When he was a student in Edinburgh, Scotland, Lord Brougham had a long discussion with a friend about the possibility of life

after death. They reached an agreement: whoever died first would try to contact the other from beyond the grave. When the two men completed their studies, they left Edinburgh and went their separate ways.

Many years later, Brougham was stepping out of his bath when he saw his old friend sitting in a chair. He noted in his diary that the event had occurred on December 19. A few days later a letter arrived from India, informing him that his friend had died—on December 19th.

Bring My Head in the House!

In the 17th century, a girl called Anne Griffiths was savagely attacked by robbers at her home. She died soon after—but not before she made a rather strange request. She asked that her head be buried in the house.

Her request was ignored and she was buried in the village churchyard. After the funeral, screams were heard in the house. The noise was terrifying. At last, the girl's body was exhumed and her skull was placed in the wall of the staircase. The screams stopped immediately, and the house has been quiet ever since.

Apparition of an Admiral

On June 22, 1893, a number of guests gathered for tea at the London home of Vice-Admiral Sir George and Lady Tyron. When the admiral, in full dress uniform, walked down the stairs and out of the door, his wife screamed in horror. The guests were also surprised, for they knew that the admiral was not supposed to have been in London at the time. Actually, he was miles away, on board his ship, the *Victoria*, off the coast of Tripoli. What none of them could possibly realize was that at that very moment the *Victoria* was going down with over half its officers and men. Sir George was among the many who perished.

The World's Most Haunted Village

Pluckley, in Kent, in the south of England, may well be the world's most haunted village. It is believed to have at least 12 ghosts and ghostly events:

1. The Red Lady—searching for her lost baby
2. The White Lady—who glides through the library of Surrenden Dering manor house
3. A horse-drawn coach that careens down the village street

4. An old pipe-smoking Gypsy woman
5. A schoolteacher who hanged himself
6. The black shape of a miller
7. A colonel who hanged himself—who walks through the woods
8. A monk—seen at a house called Greystones
9. A ghostly lady—who haunts Rose court
10. A mysterious modern ghost—who inhabits the church of St. Nicholas

In addition, terrible screams are heard near the

railway station where a man was smothered to death. And, at the appropriately named Fright Corner, the gory death of a highwayman—who was killed by a sword and speared to a tree—is said to be re-enacted every night.

The Faceless Miner

Stephen Dimbleby was a miner in Yorkshire, England. One evening in 1982, his colleagues were alarmed to see him rush out of the mine, screaming and crying. Later, Dimbleby recovered sufficiently to be able to relate what had hap-

pened. He had been in the mine, about to start his shift, when he saw a shadowy figure ahead of him. At first he thought it was another miner, but then he realized that no one else should have been in that part of the mine at that time of night. The figure was wearing a waistcoat and a grubby shirt and had an old-fashioned square helmet with a

light on it. The young miner lifted his lamp to get a better look at the man, and then froze in his tracks—the figure had no face!

Later it came out that other miners had reported similar strange sightings in that part of the mine. Then officials revealed that a miner had once been killed at that spot when he was trapped in a coal-cutting machine. At that time, miners wore exactly the type of clothing that Stephen Dimbleby had described so vividly!

The Apparition of Powis Castle

In the 18th century, the ghost of a man in a gold-laced hat often appeared in Powis Castle in Wales. He tried to communicate with the people in the castle, but no one paid him any attention. One day he appeared before a woman while she was spinning, and managed to persuade her to follow him.

He led her to a neighboring room where he instructed her to lift some floorboards. In a hole under the floorboards she discovered a heavy, locked box. She soon found the key, hidden in a crevice in the wall.

The strange man told the woman that the box

and the key must be sent to the Earl of Powis, who was, at the time, in London. The woman did as she was told, and received a handsome reward from the Earl for finding the box. No one saw the strange man in the castle ever again.

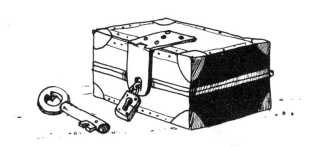

Strange Events in Gloucester Jail

At Christmas, in 1969, Robert Gore, a prisoner at Gloucester Jail in England, was so bored that he decided to play with a glass tumbler and some anagrams spread on a table.

Much to his surprise, the glass suddenly began moving of its own accord. The glass moved to several of the letters in turn and spelled out the name "Jenny Godfrey." She had been murdered at that spot in the 15th century. The spirit of Jenny then spelled out several predictions. At first the prisoners scoffed, but later, when some of the predictions came true, they began to believe in the power of their spiritual contact.

There were also incidents in which clothes and other objects were thrown around the cells at the jail. On one occasion, a prisoner reported seeing a ghostly hand in his cell. Eventually, Jenny's spirit appeared less often, but to this day strange events occur in Gloucester Jail.

The Black Dog of Blythburgh

The parson of Blythburgh in Sussex, England, was reading his sermon on August 4, 1557, when he was interrupted by a crash of thunder. A flaming arrow pierced the church wall and the church bell crashed to the ground, followed by tumbling stones. The congregation was terrified, but there was more horror to come: a great black hound of massive proportions came rushing through the church, attacking people as it went.

The hound vanished and was never seen again, but its burnt and blackened paw marks can still be seen on the old church door.

13 · Cursed!

Barney's Curse

When Barney Duffy, an Irish convict, escaped from prison on Norfolk Island off the coast of Australia, he was soon recaptured. Two soldiers who were out fishing spotted him and arrested him. All the way back to the prison Duffy cursed the soldiers. He warned them that if he should die a violent death, they too would die within a week.

The soldiers paid no attention to the convict's ravings. As soon as they returned to the prison, Duffy was hanged. Two days later the two soldiers returned to the spot where they had captured Duffy to do some fishing. Some hours later, their bodies were discovered—they been battered to death. No one ever found their attacker.

Mystery Gold Mine

In 1890, John Slumach, a Canadian Indian, discovered a gold mine in British Columbia. Before long, he was one of the richest men in the province. For a year, Johnny enjoyed a prosperous lifestyle. Then he was involved in a gun-fight. The other man died and Johnny was hanged for murder.

No one knew the exact location of Johnny's mine, but there were plenty of prospectors willing to look for it and over 20 men died in the attempt, often mysteriously. Many people believe that the mine is guarded by the spirit of the dead Indian and that he is determined that no one will ever find it and live to tell the tale.

The Mummy's Curse

In 1910, Douglas Murray bought an ancient Egyptian mummy case in Cairo. The case contained the mummified body of a princess who had lived in Thebes in 1600 B.C. Just a few hours after he purchased the case, the person who had sold it to him died mysteriously. Following this death, Douglas Murray learned that the princess had been a member of a powerful religious cult, and she had placed a dreadful curse on anyone who dared to disturb her final resting place.

Murray was an experienced Egyptologist and he had heard many stories of curses, so he paid very little attention. But then, a few days later, while on a hunting trip, his gun went off in his hands. He was so badly injured that his arm had to be amputated at the elbow. Then, on the journey back to his home in England, two of Murray's companions died suddenly. A few months later, two of his Egyptian workers also died under mysterious circumstances.

Murray decided that he must get rid of the accursed mummy case, and a woman offered to buy it from him. Almost immediately, her mother died, and then her boyfriend left her. When, eventually, she fell desperately ill, her lawyer persuaded her to return the mummy case to Douglas Murray.

Murray presented the case to the British Museum, where a photographer and an Egyptologist both suddenly died. Finally, a New York museum agreed to take the case and it was shipped to America on a new, "unsinkable" ship. The ship

was called the *Titanic*. The *Titanic* hit an iceberg and sank, taking with her almost 1,500 people— and the mummy's curse!

Ring of Death

When silent film star Rudolph Valentino bought a silver ring set with a semi-precious stone, the jeweler told him it had a reputation for bringing bad luck to its owner. Valentino scoffed at the idea and wore the ring while filming his next film, *The Young Rajah*. The film was a box-office disaster.

He put away the ring for several years. After the success of two new films, Valentino forgot about the curse on the ring and in 1926 he wore it again. Shortly afterwards, he fell ill and later died in New York.

A friend of Valentino's inherited the ring. She fell ill. But, when she passed on the ring to a young artist named Russ Colombo, she recovered from her illness almost immediately. While Colom-

bo was wearing the ring, he was killed in a car accident. So was the next owner of the ring.

The ring was then stolen and the thief was spotted by a policeman. The policeman was an excellent shot and he fired a warning in the air. As he did so, his gun slipped and the burglar was accidentally killed.

Because of its reputation, the ring was placed in a bank. The bank, which had never been robbed before, was robbed twice. In the course of one robbery, several innocent members of the public were killed.

We have no information about where the ring is now.

Diamond Curse

When the Hope Diamond was stolen from the eye of a Burmese buddha in 1688, it seems that a curse was placed on anyone who would own it. The man who stole it, French explorer Jean Baptiste Tavernier, went mad. Marie Antoinette,

who wore it, died on the guillotine. Lord Francis Hope, who acquired the diamond in 1830, gave it to his wife, who left him and died in poverty. Fifteen other owners of the Hope Diamond have died under mysterious circumstances. Even skeptics admit that these events must be more than mere coincidence.

The Curse of Tutankhamun

In 1922, four months after he and Howard Carter opened the tomb of Egyptian pharaoh Tutankhamun, Lord Caernarvon died in a Cairo hotel. At that very moment, they say, the city lights went out, and 2,000 miles away Lord Caernarvon's dog suddenly collapsed and died.

People said it was all due to the "Curse of Tutankhamun," which doomed to death anyone who tampered with his burial place.

In the ten years that followed the opening of the tomb, ten people who had some connection with

the expedition died of unnatural causes. Curse? Or coincidence?

Bull of Death

Brothers Zack and Gill Spencer were rounding up cattle in Brewster County, Texas. They began arguing over which of them owned one particularly fine-looking bull. Zack got carried away. He shot at his brother and killed him. When he realized what he had done, Zack was grief-stricken.

One of the hired hands on Zack's ranch asked how the bull should be branded. "Brand him 'murderer,' just like me," said Zack, "and then set him

loose. I hope he haunts the prairies forever." Zack then buried his brother and shot himself.

From that day in 1890, right through to about 1920, people reported seeing the bull wandering throughout the area. It was said that everyone who saw it was cursed to become a killer or be killed. Had Zack's curse come true?

14 · Strange Disappearing Acts

Desert Disappearance

When two RAF pilots, Lieutenants Day and Stewart, crashed in the Iraqi desert in 1924, rescuers rushed to the scene as fast as they could. But there was no sign of the two men. Their footprints were visible in the sand for a short distance from the wrecked plane, but then the prints suddenly stopped. The pilots were never heard of again, and no logical explanation for their disappearance has ever been given.

Disappearing Runner

James Worson was known in Leamington, England, as a fine runner. He boasted that he frequently ran the 20 miles from Leamington to Coventry. One day some of his friends called his bluff and challenged him to prove it.

On September 3, 1873, James Worson began his run, followed by two friends in a horse-drawn buggy. The athlete ran off quite happily, and the two witnesses followed. Every so often, Worson turned round to chat with his friends and to make sure they were still following him. After about five miles, Worson suddenly stumbled and let out an ear-piercing scream. The two men in the buggy saw him fall—but his body never touched the ground! He suddenly disappeared as the two gaped in disbelief. They stopped the buggy and ran to the spot where Worson had fallen. His footprints led up to the spot and then stopped. James Worson was never seen again.

Strange Disappearing Acts 109

The Vanishing Island

The island of Bouvet was named after the French Antarctic explorer, Jean Bouvet, who discovered it in 1739. According to Bouvet, the island was situated 1,500 miles from the Cape of Good Hope, South Africa, but doubts about its existence arose when two British expeditions failed to find it.

Nevertheless, in 1808 and 1822, the island seemed to be back where Jean Bouvet had said it was. British sealing vessels reported sighting it. It was marked on the maps, but then, by 1845, it had vanished again. Ten years later, it was back in position and it was still there in 1898 when a German steamer sighted it. By 1921, however, it had disappeared once more—a Norwegian survey craft, the *Stavanger*, tried to locate it unsuccessfully.

It would seem that the island of Bouvet has a will of its own. It just comes and goes as it pleases!

The Vanishing Farmer

On September 23, 1880, Judge August Peck was driving his horse and buggy near Lang's Farm outside Gallatin, Tennessee. He waved when he saw farmer David Lang in a nearby field. The farmer waved back and then suddenly disappeared. There was a scream from the farmhouse—Mrs. Lang had also witnessed the disappearance.

They rushed to the spot where David Lang had been standing. There was nothing there, and David Lang was never seen again.

The Phantom Lake

In the early 1940s the Swain family went on vacation near Beaulieu Abbey in the New Forest, England. One day they decided to go for a picnic. Driving down a country lane, looking for a good spot, they came across a lake. It was an ideal place for a picnic. In the middle of the lake, about 150 feet from shore, they saw a large stone. A magnificent sword stood on top of it.

"We thought it was some sort of memorial to King Arthur," said Mrs. Swain.

The next time they visited the New Forest, the Swains tried to find the lake, but without success.

They consulted maps of the region, but the mysterious lake was not plotted anywhere. Every three weeks or so, from that day on, the Swains together with their sons Ted and Chris searched the New Forest, looking for the lake. Over the next 17 years, they made more than 250 trips! But they

never discovered the phantom lake that they had all seen so clearly on that first visit.

Had they actually stumbled on the lake of the Arthur legend—and seen for themselves the magical sword Excalibur?

The Indian Rope Trick

India is a land of countless mysteries that have puzzled the rest of the world for centuries. Perhaps the most enduring of all these mysteries is the "Indian Rope Trick."

In the classic version of the trick, a rope is thrown into the air, where it remains rigid. A young boy then climbs up the rope only to disappear at the top. He is quickly followed by the performer, who also disappears when he reaches the top of the vertical rope. Shortly after, pieces of the boy's body fall from the sky and land on the ground at the bottom of the rope. A few seconds later, the performer is seen shinnying down the rope with a bloodstained knife in his hand.

Strange Disappearing Acts 113

On reaching firm ground the performer utters a magic word and the rope falls limp to the ground. He then gathers up the pieces of the boy's body and bundles them under a sheet. Within seconds, the sheet is lifted and the boy appears completely whole and unharmed.

This amazing trick has been described by travelers to India for over 600 years, but there is considerable doubt as to whether the trick is fact or fantasy. Magicians have put up considerable rewards to see just one performance of the trick, without success. Does the trick exist or is it just a traveler's tale?

Disappearance in Paris

A young British girl and her mother checked into an elegant hotel in Paris in May 1889. They had two single rooms.

Shortly after their arrival, the mother fell ill and a doctor was called. After examining the woman, the doctor asked the young girl to go to his office to fetch the medicine he needed. This she did, but since his office was quite far from the hotel, it was some time before she returned.

When the girl tried the door of her mother's room, it was locked. There was no answer to her repeated knocking. When she asked the manager where her mother was, he denied ever seeing her.

"I don't know anything of your mother," he said. "You arrived here alone." The girl insisted on seeing the room her mother had occupied. When the manager angrily took her into it, she saw that the room looked completely different, and a French family was now staying in it.

Back downstairs, the girl met the doctor. He denied ever meeting her or her mother. Frantically, she took her story to the British ambassador. He didn't believe her. Nor did the police. Nor did the newspapers. She never saw her mother again.

One explanation that has been set forth for this strange disappearance is that the mother died of the plague, and the hotel, fearing that people would not stay at a contaminated place, took elaborate measures to conceal the fact. But no one really knows. . . .

Biggest Disappearance?

In 1915, during World War I, the 4th Battalion of the Norfolk Regiment was fighting at a place called Gallipoli in western Turkey. The soldiers had been ordered to attack the enemy at the top of a hill. They marched up the hill, but disappeared from view into a bank of thick, low clouds. When the clouds cleared, the entire battalion had disappeared. One thousand men had vanished without trace—and were never seen again.

15 · Horror in the House

Quilt Mystery

Mrs. Florence Delfosse was sleeping at her mother's house in Poy Sippi, Wisconsin, when she was awakened by someone tugging at the quilt on her bed. She opened her eyes, but no one was in the room. Then she heard a voice cry, "Give me my Christmas quilt!" Then, for three hours, she struggled with an unseen entity that kept pulling on the quilt. Eventually, the quilt became still again, and Mrs. Delfosse was able to get back to sleep.

When she told her family of this strange occurrence, her daughter's boyfriend offered to take the quilt to his house to test it. He went home to bed, and shortly after midnight the quilt began to move.

Suddenly, there was a knock at the front door. He went downstairs to answer it. There was a strange man at the door. Although it was pouring rain, his hat and clothes were dry—and he had no face. After a few seconds the man left without saying a word.

The family never solved the mystery of the quilt. It had been found in a box in the house when Mrs. Delfosse's mother had moved there in 1972. Why it moved or who the mysterious being that wanted it back was—we'll probably never know!

Ghostly Faces on the Floor

One hot day in August 1971, at Belmez in southern Spain, an old woman was working in her kitchen. Startled by a shout from her granddaughter, she turned around to see what the trouble was and froze in horror. Staring up at her from the pink floor-tiles was a face.

The woman tried rubbing out the face with a rag, but this only resulted in the face opening its eyes wider, as if in great pain and sorrow.

The landlord of the house was called to examine the floor. He ripped up the floor-tiles and put down a new concrete floor. This seemed to solve the problem, but three weeks later, another face appeared on the new floor. The local authorities were alerted, and they decided to dig up the entire kitchen.

Workmen had not been digging long when they discovered the source of the phantom face—the kitchen floor had been covering the graveyard of a medieval monastery.

It seems that the discovery of the ancient burial ground released even more spirits. Ghostly faces began appearing all over the floor, even after new tiles had been laid. Eventually, the kitchen was locked and sealed up. But then the faces began appearing in other parts of the house.

Horror in the House   119

A team of ghost-hunters installed sound equipment, which picked up the sounds of unearthly moaning and groaning. Before a thorough investigation could be made, however, the sounds and the faces stopped, just as suddenly and mysteriously as they had started.

Oil from the Ceiling

On August 30, 1919, the Reverend Hugh Guy noticed patches of oil on some of the ceilings in his rectory in Norfolk, England. Over the next few days, the oil began to drip from the ceilings. The amount of oil seemed to be increasing every day. Then it began pouring from the walls!

Eventually, oil was said to be pouring out at the rate of two pints every ten minutes. Within a few days, about 50 gallons had accumulated.

Some investigators thought that the house was situated above an oil well and the liquid was being forced up into the house. But then it was pointed out that it was not crude oil that was flowing, but paraffin and gasoline. Eventually, without any reason anyone could see, the oil stopped flowing. The mystery has not been solved—to this day.

Blood from the Ceiling

When a U.S. farmer called Walingham discovered a skeleton in his new house in Oakville, Ohio, he threw the bones in a lime kiln. It was an action he was soon to regret. Doors in the house suddenly began to slam shut. Furniture moved mysteriously across the floor. Mysterious bells began to chime incessantly. One day, Walingham's dog started barking furiously and throwing himself about the room. It seemed the dog was being attacked by an invisible assailant, because at the end of the attack, somehow, the dog's neck was broken.

Ghostly groans were heard in the upstairs rooms of the house, and once a dismembered hand was seen floating down the staircase. When the farmer invited guests to dinner, blood appeared on the tablecloth—it was dripping from the ceiling.

Finally, the farmer and his family could stand it no longer, and they moved out of the house. No one has had the courage to live there since.

Trouble at Brockley

Samuel Trent and his family moved into their new house at Brockley in southern England in the autumn of 1920. One night in December, a neighbor knocked at the door and said that someone was switching the lights on and off in the attic rooms. Trent went up to check, but found the attic in darkness.

The following night, his daughter's bed began to shake violently. When she switched on the light the room was full of mist.

A few days later, Trent was in the living room when he heard his wife scream. He rushed upstairs to find her struggling with a pillow that was being pressed against her face by an invisible force.

In the days that followed, furniture was thrown around the rooms and deep sighs were heard. Ornaments were lifted from the shelves and smashed to the ground. Mr. Trent was attacked by something invisible, and Mrs. Trent saw a strange black figure in the hallway.

The Trents moved out of the house, and it remained empty for a year. Neighbors, however, still reported lights flashing on and off and strange bumps and knockings coming from inside the house.

In 1950, an architect moved into the house and

soon discovered the house's grisly secret—behind a false wall in the cellar were the remains of a body. It was said to have been there for 100 years. Its identity was never discovered. The body was removed and buried. The strange occurrences ceased.

Room of Terror

One evening in September 1912, George French and Donald Geary were returning to the farmhouse in County Down, Northern Ireland, where they were staying with friends. As they approached the building, they saw that one of the upstairs rooms was on fire. They rushed to the farmhouse to help.

But when they got to the house, there was no sign of any fire. The upstairs room was locked, but it was cool and no smoke was coming from it.

When the farmer, Mark Donague, came home, he told the men: "That room is haunted, so we always keep it locked. The last person to go in there was one of my farm workers, ten years ago.

The first I knew of it was when we heard a scream. We rushed upstairs as he staggered out of the room clutching his throat. Something in that room had tried to strangle him. The key to the room has remained in my desk drawer ever since."

The following afternoon, when Donague was out, George and Donald took the key and went up to the room.

Apart from the fact that it was dusty and the furniture was decaying, the room seemed quite ordinary. Donald Geary walked in. George French followed. Suddenly the temperature dropped and a glowing ball of pink light appeared over the rocking chair in the middle of the room. The ball of light grew larger and larger, until the whole room appeared bathed in a bright fire. The furniture began to vibrate and the rocking chair was swaying back and forth.

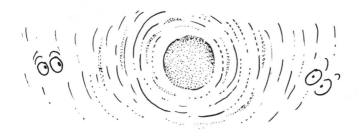

Suddenly Donald grabbed his neck and screamed. Something was trying to strangle him.

He struggled desperately with the unseen force that was pushing him down to the floor. George rushed over to help his friend. As he pulled him to the door, the glow diminished and the room became warm again.

As Donald recovered in the corridor, George locked the door. They returned the key to the desk drawer and vowed never to be so skeptical again.

Index